A Heroine for all Seasons!

For Freya, Ava and Aina. And a big thank you to Alfredo
(for the racing pigeon) – *MF*

To my friends Julien, Nolwenn and their little Lisa. To all
the people who love running barefoot in the rain and
splashing in puddles – *JD*

STRIPES PUBLISHING
An imprint of Magi Publications
1 The Coda Centre, 189 Munster Road, London SW6 6AW

A paperback original
First published in Great Britain in 2009

Text copyright © Maeve Friel, 2009
Illustrations copyright © Joelle Dreidemy, 2009

The right of Maeve Friel and Joelle Dreidemy to be identified as the
author and illustrator of this work respectively has been asserted by
them in accordance with the Copyright, Designs and Patents Act, 1988.

ISBN: 978-1-84715-084-4

A CIP catalogue record for this book is available from the British Library.

Printed and bound in the UK

10 9 8 7 6 5 4 3 2 1

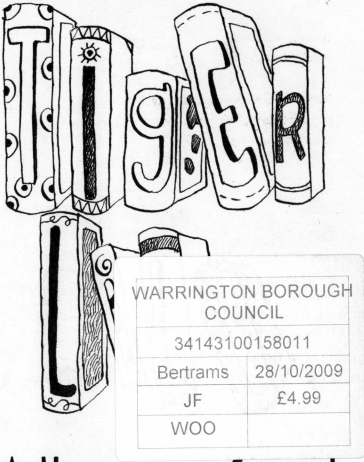

TIGER LILY

A Heroine for all Seasons!

Maeve Friel

Illustrated by
Joelle Dreidemy

Stripes

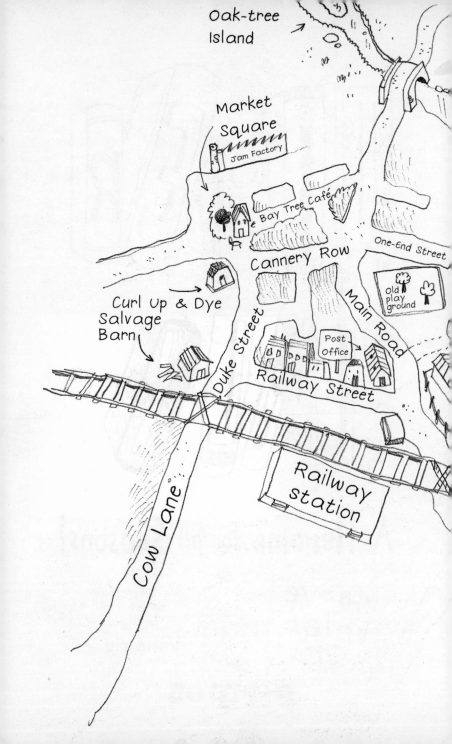

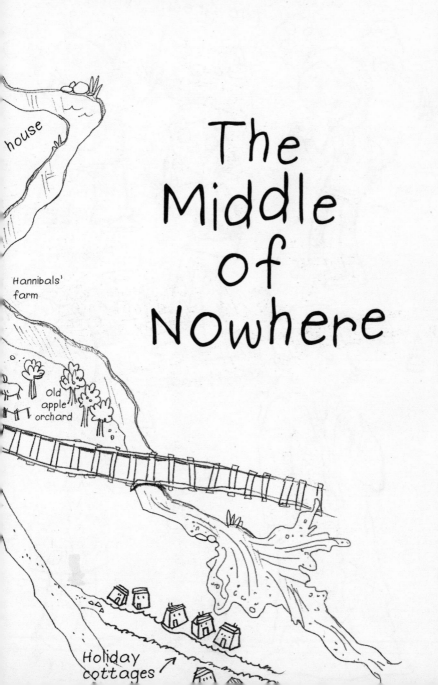

house

Hannibals'
farm

old
apple
orchard

The
Middle
of
Nowhere

Holiday
cottages

Tiger Lily and the Evacuees on the Night of the Great Wind

Me

Streaky Bacon Junior

Psammy

Nick

Granny Rita

Smoky Bacon

Lauren

Sweetness and Light

Rosie

Mum

Chapter 1

It was a dark and stormy morning in The Middle of Nowhere. Raindrops drummed on the rooftops. The blackboard outside Granny's café flew away and clattered down Cannery Row. Chilly winds whisked the leaves off the apple trees and rattled the bedroom windows on One-End Street.

Tiger Lily tugged her duvet higher around her shoulders and turned over a page of her library book.

"Don't you just love Saturdays, Rosie? Let's not even think about getting up until

I finish my book, *Five Children and It*. I've just got to the bit where burglars have broken in and taken Lady Chittenden's diamonds!"

Rosie the greyhound flicked an ear to show she had got the message, rolled over until her three legs were pointing at the ceiling and went back to sleep.

Two pages later, there was a terrible crash and the sound of breaking glass.

Crash! Bang! Smash!

A muffled scream came from the direction of Mum's room.

"Lily! Help!"

With one heroic leap, Tiger was out of bed and bounding to the rescue, with Rosie hopping along behind her.

She raced down the corridor and flung open Mum's bedroom door.

"Mum!" she shrieked. "Where are you? What's happened?"

The room looked as if a tornado had hit it. The bookcase had toppled over and hundreds of books lay strewn across the carpet. Heaps of dresses were piled up on the bed. Silk saris in brilliant jewel colours spilled out of suitcases, along with a tangle

of national flags and a fake fur coat. Walking boots, high heels, slippers and a pair of black rubber flippers were scattered around the floor. A scarlet ski suit was slung on a chair, a fluffy pantomime cat costume dangled from the central ceiling light and, hanging over the bedposts, there were two straw safari hats and a tasselled fez.

"Mum?" Tiger called again.

An icy draught of cold air lifted the curtains and made them billow out.

"Yikes! Don't move, Rosie, the windowpane is broken. There might be glass on the floor. Mum! Where are you? We've been burgled! Call the police!"

Tiger stuck her feet into the rubber flippers, flapped across the room and looked out of the broken window to see if she could catch the robbers making their getaway.

Unfortunately, there weren't any robbers making a run for it, but there was a lake where the garden had been and a procession of flowerpots floating around the shed like a family of ducks. Even more amazing, the little stream that ran behind the house was a raging torrent. It had burst its banks and was swirling around the muddy knees of the cattle in the field opposite.

"Mum!" she roared. "Come quick. The Middle of Nowhere is drowning."

Behind her there was a little tapping noise, and a small voice, which seemed to

come from the wardrobe, said, "Everything's fine, sweetheart, just let me out."

"Mum?"

Tiger Lily yanked open the door and Mum fell out.

For some inexplicable reason, she was wearing a pair of enormous ski goggles and a Moroccan jellaba.

"Mum," said Tiger, pulling her to her feet, "what's happened? Are you all right? Were you hiding from the robbers? Why are you in disguise?"

"I wasn't hiding…" Mum turned a little red. "…I was rummaging in the wardrobe, looking for an old raincoat, and I kept finding things and trying them on, and then the wind blew the window open and the bookcase fell over and the wardrobe door slammed against my bottom … and the next thing I knew, I was locked in."

"No robbers, then?" Tiger said, sounding rather disappointed. "I was kind of wishing something exciting would happen. By the way, have you ever tasted sago pudding? Or mutton hash? The children in my book eat the strangest stuff—"

"Hang on, Lil…" Mum interrupted. "Look what Rosie's done. She's wearing my veil."

Tiger spun round. Rosie had jumped up on to the bed and nuzzled under the clutter to settle down for a nap. She looked up at Tiger from beneath a pretty white scarf fringed with gold coins.

"Did you say your veil? When did you need a veil?"

"Oh, it was ages ago when I did a belly-dancing course in Turkey. It's real silk, you know." Mum put the veil on her head and made little rippling movements with her tummy. The gold coins tinkled.

Tiger Lily looked appalled. "Why on earth do you keep all this weird stuff, Mum? You're not going to be doing belly dancing again, are you?"

17

"It's not weird, Lily. Most of this stuff is vintage: it never goes out of fashion."

Tiger hooted. "That jellaba was never *in* fashion..."

"...but I bought it in Casablanca..."

"...and where did that awful ski suit come from? I didn't know you could ski."

"Oh yes – I wore that the first time I went skiing in Italy. My whole life is in this wardrobe, Lily. Look – those were the safari hats I bought in Kenya. And this was my flag collection of the countries I visited – Australia, Japan, Chile ... so many memories..."

The coins around her face tinkled.

Tiger Lily reached for the veil, draped it over her head and looked at herself in the mirror.

"You know what?" said Mum. "It suits you. You look like Scheherazade."

"Who's Scheherazade?"

"Oh, Lily, you would love Scheherazade. Would you like to hear a story?" She cleared a space on the bed beside Rosie and they sat down.

The Story of Princess Scheherazade and the One Thousand and One Arabian Nights

As told by Mum to Tiger Lily On the Day of the Great Winds

Once upon a time, there was a king of Arabia who was terribly, terribly jealous. Every night he would take a different wife, but then he would kill her at dawn. So when he chose Princess Scheherazade for his bride, she knew her life was in danger. It was just as well that she also knew that there is nothing as powerful as a good story.

On the night of her wedding, Princess Scheherazade told the king story after story, weaving stories within stories so that the story never ended. When dawn broke, she had reached such an interesting bit that the king spared her life so that she could

finish the story the next night. And she did the same thing that night and the next night and went on spinning stories within stories about genies and talking animals and wizards and flying carpets for one thousand and one nights, one after the other.

And, of course, by that time, the king was madly in love with her and couldn't bear the idea of killing her and they lived happily ever after.

And everybody, even people who have never heard of Scheherazade and never read books, like your friend Sammy, knows some of the stories that Scheherazade made up, like *Sinbad the Sailor* and *Aladdin and the Wonderful Lamp* and *Ali Baba and The Forty Thieves.*

Mum says: an essential read for people who love stories.

"So, you see," Mum said, "telling stories literally saved Scheherazade's life."

"I have to read that book, Mum," Tiger declared. "Have you got it?"

"It's here somewhere."

Mum cast an eye over the spilled books. Outside, the wind blew harder. The window banged. The pantomime cat costume fell off the light.

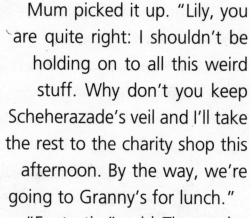

Mum picked it up. "Lily, you are quite right: I shouldn't be holding on to all this weird stuff. Why don't you keep Scheherazade's veil and I'll take the rest to the charity shop this afternoon. By the way, we're going to Granny's for lunch."

"Fantastic," said Tiger, who loved Granny and also loved going to charity shops to look for second-hand books. "I'll help you clear up."

"I do wish I could find my old raincoat though. It's a sort of zebra print, very striking ... I bought it in New York..." Mum's face took on a dreamy faraway look. "I remember it was a very wet autumn day, just like today, and Auntie Pamela and I were going to see *A Masked Ball*. You know how Pam loves opera..."

And Mum started singing.

"Mum, you're as mad as a hatter. Just look at yourself in the mirror."

"You're one to talk," Mum said, and they both burst out laughing.

Chapter 2

It took Tiger and her mum all morning to
clear up the broken glass, block up the
window, put back the books, tidy up the
room and sort out the clothes. It shouldn't
have taken quite so long, but Tiger Lily found
One Thousand and One Arabian Nights
under the bed and started to read it.

All the time, the weather got worse. The
wind kept howling and the rain came in
through the ceiling and they had to put
buckets all over the place to catch the drips.
Even though it was daytime, it was as dark

24

as night, and when Mum went to turn on the lights, she discovered there was a power cut. The whole village was in darkness.

Then, as Tiger Lily was dragging the last bag of clothes downstairs, the telephone rang. She propped the bag on the kitchen counter beside the fridge and picked up the phone.

It was Granny Rita and she didn't sound at all happy.

"What's keeping you? I'm all at sixes and sevens. Streaky Bacon is driving me crazy. He's supposed to be fixing up a temporary electricity generator for me, but all he's interested in is getting the telly to work so he and Spanners can watch the horse racing. Lunch is ready. Tell your Mum—"

25

The rest of what she said was drowned out by a long whistle as the 13:25 train trundled across the railway bridge. Rashers Bacon, the driver, always slowed down in case any of the cows or peacocks from Hannibals' farm were wandering on the track.

"It's the train!" Tiger shouted over the noise. "I forgot. It's a Sammy weekend. I said I'd meet him."

(Sammy was Tiger Lily's best friend and Trusty Companion. Every other weekend he came from the city to stay with his dad, Nick the Chippie.)

"Why don't you tell Nick and Sammy to come for lunch, too?" said Granny. "They won't want to sit at home in the dark."

"OK. Got to go, Granny. See you later."

Tiger grabbed her coat and bag.

"Bye, Mum. I'm off to meet Sammy at the station," she shouted. "See you in the café. Bye, Rosie, be good."

As she made for the front door, she caught a glimpse of herself in the hall mirror and stuffed her veil in her coat pocket.

The train had already pulled into the station when Tiger splashed into Railway Street. A stranger in a floppy poppy hat was coming through the turnstile. She held a big umbrella in one hand and a carpet bag in the other. At the pavement, she stopped, pulled her hat down over her ears, looked left and right, and waded across the road. As she passed Tiger, a sudden squall of wind caught her unawares and blew her umbrella inside out.

"*Mamma Mia!*" she exclaimed. "What a windy day. Hold this, will you."

She thrust her bag into Tiger's arms and turned around to lean into the wind, alternately clutching at her floppy hat and struggling with the inside-out brolly.

"If you're not careful," said Tiger, eyeing the woman's coat and the poppy on her hat and her carpet bag, "you could fly up

and away like Mary Poppins."

The woman gave her a strange look, pulled her hat down sharply over her ears and, this time, won the battle with the brolly, which sprang back the right way round.

"Spit spot," she said, holding out a hand for her bag.

Tiger hurried into the station, grinning broadly.

Tiger Lily's Book Reports

Mary Poppins
by P.L. Travers

Mary Poppins is a mysterious lady who blows in on the wind and becomes the nanny for the Banks children. Sometimes she makes their life very exciting and magical, like when they visit her uncle Mr Wigg for tea and they all laugh so much that they float up to the ceiling – but she is not always nice. She can be very cross and bossy and she always has the last word. Like "spit spot", which means, "Hurry up, chop chop!"

If you have only seen the film, you might be a bit surprised by the Mary Poppins books. For example, in one of the stories in *Mary Poppins in the Park*, Michael Banks is cross and grumpy and wishes he was miles away from everywhere so Mary Poppins puts a spell on him to teach him a lesson. He ends up in outer space on the Cat Star where he has a very frightening time.

But it serves him right because anybody who's ever read anything knows that you have to be very careful what you wish for. But I liked the story anyway because I like cats and there is a cat princess in it called Tiger-Lily!

If you have not read the Mary Poppins books, you should.

I give this book: 4 parrot umbrellas

Chapter 3

When Tiger blew into the station, Sammy and his dad were making slow headway along the platform, hand in hand. Their bodies were hunched over and they held their heads down like battering rams against the rain. The wind was screaming like a thousand toddlers having a tantrum all at the same time.

"I've just seen Mary Poppins," Tiger yelled at Sammy.

"The film?" Sammy yelled back.

"No, the real person, the one in the book," Tiger cried. "Shall I tell you about it?"

"No!" shouted Sammy, who never read books if he could help it.

"I have my book report right here in my bag," Tiger shouted back helpfully.

"NO!" Sammy roared.

"Why are you so grumpy?" Tiger roared back.

Sammy's dad took Lily by his free hand. "Maybe it's not a good time for book reports, Tiger. Come on, guys, let's get out of the rain. RUN!"

The lights of Granny Rita's café shone brightly in the gloom of Market Square. Sammy and Nick and Tiger crashed through the door and stood gasping to catch their breath.

Streaky Bacon Junior was slumped at a corner table by the window.

He looked up and scowled.

"What's the matter with you?" asked Tiger. Streaky dribbled some salt into the sugar bowl. "I've been grounded," he said, "again."

"What did you do this time?"

"Nothing, absolutely nothing," said Streaky. He added a bit of black pepper into his mix. "I just did a drawing and sprayed 'Beware of the Wolves' on the post office wall and wrote my name in TINY writing." (The Wolves were the bad-tempered twins who ran The Middle of Nowhere post office.) "And it was a good drawing, not scribbling, like my dad says. It's ART."

He looked daggers at his father, who was standing on a stepladder behind the counter waving an old-fashioned television aerial at the set on the wall. But Streaky Senior wasn't paying any attention. He was listening to Spanners Murphy the cowboy plumber, who was sitting on the counter reading out the odds for the afternoon's racing.

Spanners politely tipped his hat at the new arrivals.

"Howdy doody, y'all. Discombobulating weather, that's for sure," he drawled.

The television suddenly made a terrible hissing noise. Everybody covered their ears and Granny Rita click-clacked out from the kitchen, brandishing a soup ladle.

Spanners jumped off the counter like a cat that had just stepped on a hot tin roof and folded up his newspaper.

"Spanners, I'm telling you the racing is off, O-F-F, cancelled, not on," Granny told him. "And Streaky, for the last time, I need you to get off that ladder and put it away. I'm expecting a lot of people for lunch."

Streaky Senior waggled the rabbit ears of the aerial at the television. "Just two minutes, Rita, pet ... me and Spanners have an accumulator."

"Don't call me pet," said Granny, giving the stepladder a violent whack with her ladle.

As Streaky Senior wobbled backwards, the television set boomed into life and a voice announced, "...and finally, news is just coming in of an incident at the City Zoo, where high winds have broken the glass roof of the aviary and hundreds of exotic birds, mostly *Psittacidae*, have flown away. We're going over to the zoo for more information..." The television screen became a hissing white blizzard again, and the newsreader vanished.

"Wow! Does anybody know what kind of birds they were, those sittywhatsits?" asked Tiger.

"The word is *Psittacidae*," said Streaky Junior.

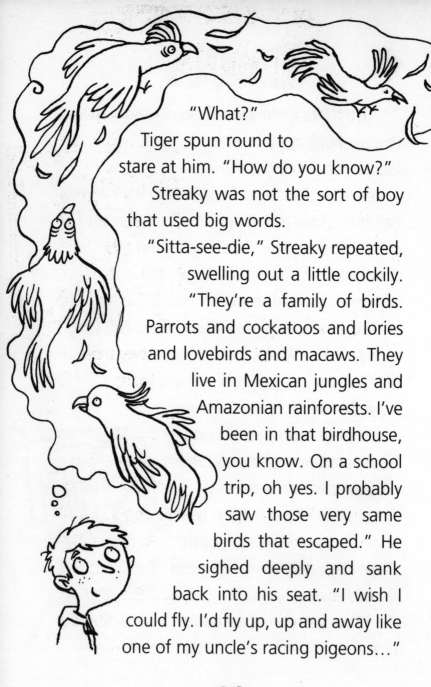

"What?"
Tiger spun round to stare at him. "How do you know?"

Streaky was not the sort of boy that used big words.

"Sitta-see-die," Streaky repeated, swelling out a little cockily. "They're a family of birds. Parrots and cockatoos and lories and lovebirds and macaws. They live in Mexican jungles and Amazonian rainforests. I've been in that birdhouse, you know. On a school trip, oh yes. I probably saw those very same birds that escaped." He sighed deeply and sank back into his seat. "I wish I could fly. I'd fly up, up and away like one of my uncle's racing pigeons…"

38

The three children turned and looked out at the soggy grey skies and  the rain bouncing off the pavements. There wasn't a single parrot to be seen, not even a pigeon. The only sign of life was a scar-faced cat that streaked across the square and scuttled up the trunk of the bay tree.

"What a pity!" Tiger said. "No sittywhatsits."

"*Psittacidae*," Streaky repeated. He rolled the word and let it melt on his tongue like a square of delicious dark chocolate. "Sitta-see-die – it's got a silent p, you know."

"Oh," exclaimed Tiger. "I know about silent ps, too. In the book I'm reading, there's a stone-age fairy called a Psammead. It's pronounced 'Sammyadd' with a silent p at the start, and he eats Megatheriums."

She rummaged in her bag and brought out her library book with a flourish. "Here it is – *Five Children and It*! The best thing about the IT is that it can grant wishes."

Sammy held up a hand. "Tiger! No! I cannot listen to book reports when I am cold and wet and I have an empty stomach and what on earth are megatheriums, and Dad, can I have sausages and chips, please?"

Tiger snapped her book shut. "You know something, Sammy. You remind me of the Psammead. It didn't like being wet either and it was extremely rude and grumpy. From now on, I am going to call you Psammy with a silent p, especially because you look just like a Psammead when you are hammering your drums."

40

"Who cares," Sammy said crossly, "if the p is silent anyway!" He marched off and sat down beside Streaky Junior.

Nick cleared his throat to fill the awkward silence. "I'd love a bowl of soup, please, Rita," he said.

"...and I could murder a cup of tea and a cherry scone," Spanners said, looking up from the *Racing Post*. "When you have time," he added hastily, as Granny picked up her ladle.

Tiger moved over to the corner table. "I'm sorry if I offended you, Psammy. Please don't be discombobulated. You are my Trusty Companion after all. As well as being the best drummer in the whole world."

Sammy rolled his eyes. "Oh, go on then, tell us about the Sammyadd..."

But before Tiger could explain any more, the door blew open again and in came a noisy gaggle of people.

First there was Mum, in an appalling raincoat, and Auntie Pamela with her hair in a state, and Auntie Pamela's Polish boyfriend, Piotr, who immediately got his long stripy scarf tangled in the door handle.

The scar-faced cat that had been sheltering in the tree saw its chance and shot in the door.

"Hi, Mum," said Mum. "I'd love some of your Tuscan Bean Soup. It smells fantastic."

"And Piotr and I'll have a green tea and a skinny latte. And two pierogi."

"As I was going to say…" Tiger started again, but just then a nose-puckering whiff of wet cow snuck in under the door and the Hannibals from Hannibals' farm barged in, in their vast, smelly waterproofs.

"A toasted cheese sandwich with a side order of chips, please," Mr Hannibal bellowed.

"And some of your lovely soup and a slice of Pizza Pinocchio," Mrs Hannibal bellowed louder.

"I don't believe it," Tiger said furiously. "It's just like the beginning of *The Hobbit*, when all the dwarves arrive, two by two, and start asking for cake and beer and everyone has to be fed before Gandalf arrives—"

Suddenly, Auntie Pamela let out a piercing operatic shriek and pointed outside.

"They're flying!"

Aa-Aa-Aa-Aa-Aa

A chorus line of five flapping figures was blowing across the square, clinging to each other.

From left to right, they were the ancient Wolf twins, clutching each other, Lauren Schultz, clinging on to her dad's arm and, at the front, Streaky Junior's granddad, Smoky Bacon.

Tiger Lily, Granny, Auntie Pamela, Mrs Hannibal and Spanners rushed to hold the door open and haul them all into the café.

The scar-faced cat made a beeline for the kitchen.

"Oh, Tiger!" said Lauren breathlessly. "Did you see how the wind lifted us off the ground? Was that our cat, Harry? Can I have a milkshake, please?"

The Wolf twins, Sweetness and Light, who were anything but sweet or light by nature, looked as if they were about to blow their tops. They narrowed their eyes at Streaky Junior until he slid so far down his chair that he was nearly under the table. They snapped their umbrellas shut and shook raindrops all over the floor.

"A round of egg sandwiches, please," growled the first Wolf, who could have been Sweetness.

"And a good old-fashioned pot of tea," growled the second, who might have been Light.

"We don't want any of those new-fangled tea bags…"

"…and we like our tea strong."

Granny gave Tiger a wink. "Tea you can trot a mouse on coming up, ladies."

"And two sausage rolls, love," said Smoky.

"Now," Tiger Lily said when everyone had settled down, "can I please read you my book report?"

For the umpteenth time the door banged open.

47

"Gracious to goodness! What a gale! I found this clattering around on Cannery Row!"

A woman in a floppy poppy hat stood in the doorway, holding Granny's blackboard in her arms.

"Mary Poppins!" Tiger exclaimed.

TIGERLAND

"Gee," said the woman, staring at the book Tiger was holding, "am I interrupting your reading group? If I can just find somewhere to sit, I'd love to know what you're reading."

That was all Tiger Lily needed to hear. She rushed to take the blackboard from the woman, found a place for her carpet bag, helped her off with her coat and gallantly offered her the window seat where Streaky Bacon Junior had been sitting.

"Now," said the new arrival, as she elegantly peeled off her gloves, finger by finger, "off you go. We are all ears."

Tiger Lily hopped up on the counter and began to read.

Tiger Lily's Book Reports
As told to the Customers in the Bay Tree Cáfe on the Day of the Great Wind

Five Children and It by E. Nesbit

The It in this story is a Psammead, a sort of furry and very grumpy stone-age sand fairy that lives in a gravel pit and has eyes that can stand out at the end of long stalks like a snail. The best thing about a Psammead is that it has the power to grant wishes. Unfortunately, the five children in the story keep making silly or accidental wishes that just land them in trouble. I mean, imagine wishing for a gravel-pit full of gold coins!

As if they could spend gold coins in an ordinary shop! No wonder they were nearly arrested. They should have known that you have to be careful what you wish for.

This book was written quite a long time ago so the children say things like "spiffing" when they mean "fantastic" and "in a frightful stew" when they mean "in big trouble". The other interesting thing about this book is that they are always hungry like my friend Sammy, but they eat strange "grub" that I have never heard of like sago pudding and disgusting things like boiled rabbit.

I say – jolly spiffing!
I give this book: 5 Psammeads

Chapter 4

Miss Monica Caramelo, for that was the name of the new arrival, was American. "This is my first trip to Europe," she told everyone when Tiger finished her book report and they were introducing themselves. "My daddy's side of the family came from The Middle of Nowhere back in the last century."

"Caramelo?" said Mum doubtfully. Mum was a librarian and knew all about family trees. "I don't think you'll find any Caramelos round here."

Miss Caramelo laughed a silvery laugh.

"Oh my, I should have said, Caramelo is my stage name... I'm an actress, just like my momma and poppa. I was born and raised, as they say, in a theatrical basket. We run a little theatre in..." and she said a name, and all the grown-ups nodded as if they had heard of it even though they hadn't.

Tiger Lily was over the moon. "Imagine being born and raised in a theatrical basket!" she whispered to Sammy. "I could be a different person night after night instead of being just me, stuck in The Middle of Nowhere."

Sammy shuddered, remembering the green tights and the ridiculous hat he had to wear the last time Tiger made him go on the stage. "Don't get any of your ideas, Tiger. I am not dressing up. I do not want to be on the stage ever again."

"Oh, Psammy," said Tiger, "you don't have to be an actor to be on the stage. You could be a musician with fans from all over the world."

"I wish!" Sammy hammered out a beat on the table with his knife and fork until Nick told him to stop.

Tiger turned to Miss Caramelo, her eyes shining. "You know, we have a little theatre here too. It's called the Old Jam Factory and it opened on Midsummer Night and I was Titania and Sammy was Puck…"

Sammy gave her a sharp kick under the table.

"Really?" Miss Caramelo said. "My grandpoppa would love to know that The Middle of Nowhere has its own theatre."

The Wolf twins looked down their sharp noses and pursed their thin lips.

"It's nothing to write home about," said Sweetness (or it might have been Light). "It's just an old factory that's supposed to be a community hall…"

"…except," said Light (or it might have been Sweetness), "it looks like a second-hand furniture shop…"

"…and the plumbing doesn't work."

Streaky Bacon's cheeks blazed and Spanners nervously rattled his cowboy boots against the bar stool, but Mum gave the twins a bright smile and said between gritted teeth, "But it's all thanks to our benefactors,

55

Streaky Bacon and Spanners, that we have the theatre in the first place because they did it up at their own expense and in their own time for us all to enjoy…"

The twins sniffed.

"You know something," said Miss Caramelo, thoughtfully stirring a teaspoonful of sugar into her coffee, "you could hire that hall out as a film location. Why, back home we make a whole heap of money hiring out our theatre for film shoots and there's always work for extras. I could possibly put in a word for you with some of my European contacts."

"Mmmmm…"

The café became suddenly quiet as everybody thought about being in a film.

56

"But now, you kind people must excuse me, I have got to find myself somewhere to stay for the night before this storm gets any worse. Is there a bed and breakfast place in The Middle of Nowhere?"

"I'd be thrilled to put you up," Auntie Pamela said, with her most charming smile. "I have a lovely room above the salon..." Her voice trailed off, "but there's no electricity..."

"And we have a guest room in our farmhouse," said Mrs Hannibal, "but we're already up to our knees in flood water ... the cows are quite waterlogged..."

"That is a real shame." Monica started to gather her belongings together. "I guess I'd better get the train back to the city and visit you good people another time when the weather is kinder."

"Unfortunately…" Smoky Bacon pulled his watch out of his waistcoat pocket and looked at it with a worried frown. "Unfortunately," he repeated, "the only train out of The Middle of Nowhere today has been cancelled, owing to water on the tracks. There won't be another train until tomorrow at the earliest."

He gave Miss Caramelo an apologetic smile.

"Oh, jiminy! What am I going to do?" Miss Caramelo clasped her hands to her heart.

"What a frightful stew!" Tiger said, clasping her hands to her heart.

Then she had one of her ingenious ideas.

"I know," she said. "Granny has electricity! Why don't you stay right here in Granny's spare room? Then tomorrow I can show you our theatre and Mum can research your family tree and you can tell your European contacts all about us."

Tiger and Monica Caramelo looked at Granny and Mum. Their mouths had formed two perfectly round Os.

"Oh!" Mum said and gave Lily a look.

"Oh!" said Granny. "What a *spiffing* plan!"

Miss Caramelo clapped her hands delightedly and sat down again. "That is so kind of you. In that case, I will have my coffee."

As she raised her cup to her lips, Streaky Junior gave a sort of strangled yelp that sounded like "salt" and looked despairingly at Tiger.

Tiger got the message.

She made a spectacular flying leap off the counter, sending the blackboard clattering on to the floor, and grabbed the cup out of Miss Caramelo's hands.

"No, no!" she shouted, rather more loudly than she meant to. "Forget your coffee. It's probably cold anyway."

"Absolutely!" Granny came out from behind the counter and gave Streaky Junior

a ferociously hard stare as she picked up Miss Caramelo's carpet bag.

"Would you like to run upstairs with me and see your room, Miss Caramelo?"

"It would be a pleasure, Miss Rita," Miss Caramelo replied, "but, you know, we Caramelos do not run. At all times, we are cool, calm and collected. And do call me Miss Monica. Why, we might even be family!"

Chapter 5

As soon as Miss Rita and Miss Monica went off to see the spare room, the café broke out in excited chatter.

"Imagine if they made a film right here in The Middle of Nowhere!" Auntie Pamela was burbling with excitement. "I could be the official hairdresser. I can see my name already, rolling up on the credits."

With special thanks to
Pamela of **Curl Up & Dye.**
Hairdresser to the Stars.

"You're already a star in my eyes, my little sugar plum," Piotr assured her.

Tiger and Sammy rolled their eyes.

"If we all got work as extras," said Spanners, "and pooled our money, we could put a new dance floor in the Old Jam Factory. For line dancing..." His cowboy boots rattled against the bar stool more cheerfully this time. "Doing the Cajun Walk, yee hi!"

"And we could have a big screen," said Streaky, "for the footie and the race nights."

"I'd better plant up some more hanging baskets," said Smoky, "to make a good impression before these European contacts arrive."

Mum put up a hand. "Whoa, people! Don't count your chickens … we don't know who this woman is. She may just be some old ham showing off. Have any of you ever heard of … um, where did she say she was from?"

But nobody paid any attention. The glamour of the film business had gone to all their heads.

Tiger Lily was thrilled. "For once, everyone is acting sensibly," she told Sammy. "Let's make up a new menu for Granny for the film crew. Do you think they would like Grilled Megatherium? Or could that be some sort of extinct dinosaur that only Psammeads ate? I'll put Boiled Rabbit with Onions, too."

"Tiger, hang on a minute; maybe your mum's right..." Sammy began, just as the television came back to life with a deafening boom.

"Welcome to *It's a Wind-Up*," shouted an excited voice. "It's the final showdown between the Welsh Dragon and the Russian Bear."

The camera cut to a circus tent where two strongmen with thick necks and one-shouldered leotards were showing off their rippling muscles and baring their teeth in mock scowls. They were pulling two huge trucks with thick cables tied to their waists.

At the CRACK of a starting pistol, they were OFF, staggering around the arena, dragging their trucks behind them. The audience – there weren't very many of them – gave half-hearted cheers.

"Psammy," said Tiger, "I have another idea. Why don't we hold a traditional fair the day the film people come, like the ones in Mary Poppins' day? You can be THE SILENT P: Psammy the Pstrongman. Mum probably has some old leotard you can borrow…"

Sammy looked terrified. He stared at her, speechless, mostly because his mouth was full of sausage but, before he could swallow, Tiger carried on.

"…and I will be Tiger Lil, the gypsy fortune-teller, because I have the gypsy headscarf already and I'm brilliant at knowing what is going to happen."

Sammy's eyebrows shot up under his cap. "Tiger, you never know what is going to happen." He started to count on his fingers. "One, you didn't know that the river was going to flow in the wrong direction when we were on the pallet raft. Two, you didn't know that the Hannibals' boars had escaped to Oak Tree Island during the Boar Wars. Three…"

Tiger stopped him. "But I knew Miss Monica was going to drink the coffee with the sugar that Streaky had put salt and pepper in…"

Streaky Junior rubbed the stubbly black hairs of his newly-sprouted moustache. Even though Tiger was a girl, and a very bossy girl at times, she was all right. "Yeah, cheers, Tiger," he mumbled. "You know, I could be in your fair, too, if you like. I'm a bird mimic. Listen!" And he whistled, "lu lu lü lü li li – that's a nightingale."

"Can you speak BIRD?" exclaimed Lauren and Tiger together, but before Streaky could answer, another loud CRACK made them all jump. This time it was not the starting pistol on the telly.

It was a huge thunderclap. It crashed over the village, toppling telephone poles and setting every dog barking. At the same time, a bright flash of lightning lit up the square. The television strongmen disappeared in a puff of smoke. The generator made a strangled noise (never to work again) and the lights went out.

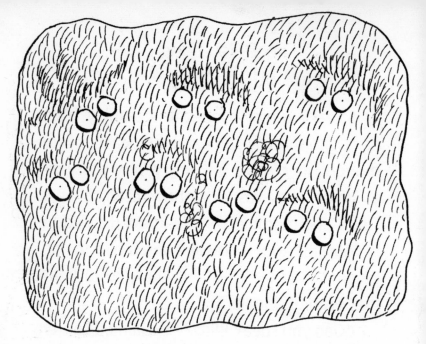

"Lawks almighty," drawled Spanners in the darkness, "it must be time for us all to batten down the hatches."

"What are hatches? What does batten mean?" Lauren piped up.

"Mum! Where are you?" said Tiger. "I need to go home. I think I can hear Rosie barking."

"It's time we all went home," said Smoky, checking his watch. "I've got a pigeon to see to."

"And I need to feed the cat," said Lauren.

The Bay Tree Café

Introducing Granny Rita's New HISTORIC Grub as featured in
Five Children and It!

Today's Special – Grilled Megatherium
(not available if extinct)

Cold Mutton Hash and Greens

Boiled Rabbit with Onions

Cold Pressed Tongue

The Puddings

Sago Pudding
(not suitable for children)

Suet roly-poly

YEUCH!

SPIFFING NOT!

Chapter 6

When Tiger Lily and Mum got back to One-End Street, Rosie was fast asleep on the couch, out for the count, not the teensiest bit upset by the thunder.

Mum battened down the hatches, which turned out to mean lighting candles and drawing the curtains to keep out the sound and fury of the storm, but even with the hatches battened down, the howling and battering and rumbling never stopped. Tiles tumbled off the roof and the plastic sheet at the broken window ripped itself apart and

took off for Hannibals' farm. The buckets they'd put down to catch the drips overflowed, and no matter how fast they worked to empty them, more jumbo-sized leaks kept appearing. In no time at all, every room upstairs was awash and they had run out of buckets and basins and bowls.

To make matters worse, while they were upstairs dealing with the leaks from the roof, flood water silently, sneakily, poured under the back door and when they came downstairs, *everywhere* was awash.

"That's it! I'm throwing in the towel," said Mum, wading into the kitchen and rescuing Rosie's bowl, which was bobbing about under the table. "We shall have to evacuate."

"Evacuate!" Tiger yelped. "You mean, like in *Carrie's War,* when Carrie and her brother were sent away so they couldn't be bombed and all they had was a little suitcase and a label round their necks? Are you sending me away on the next train? Can Sammy come with me? Where shall I find a gas mask? What shall I wear?"

Mum silently counted to ten.

"Don't be silly, Lily!" she said. "It's only weather, not a war. You really must stop all these crazy ideas. Honestly, the more you

74

read, the madder you become."

She snapped off a bag from a roll of bin liners. "I'm not sending you away anywhere and anyway, the trains aren't running. Evacuating just means we need to get out of the house and find somewhere dry and safe for the night. Let's pack a change of clothes and some candles and yummy food and we'll go round to Pamela's."

"Fantastic!" said Tiger. "And while we're evacuating, I'll tell you about *Carrie's War*."

Tiger Lily's Book Reports
As told to Mum on the Day of the Great Wind

Carrie's War by Nina Bawden

This book happens in wartime when Carrie and her brother are sent out of London to be safe from the bombs. They have to live with scaredy-cat Auntie Lou and her brother Mr Evans, who is a bully and keeps barking, "Don't you know there's a war on?" There is another evacuee called Albert Sandwich, who is staying with Mr Evans's sister, Mrs Gotobed, who lives in Druid's Bottom with Mr Johnny and their housekeeper Hepzibah. (This book is full of people with funny names.) Mrs Gotobed and her brother Mr Evans have not spoken to each other for years and when Mrs Gotobed dies, Mr Evans does a cruel and mean thing, but you will have to read the book yourself if you want to know more.

I liked Carrie's War because it made me feel I was reading a true story.

I give this book: 10 stars

Tiger Lily was putting a box of dog biscuits in the bag of overnight stuff when Mum's mobile phone rang. She put the bag on the kitchen counter and went to answer it. A hysterical voice sobbed at the other end.

"SOS. Mayday! Mayday! Is that you, Vicky? Come at once."

"It's me, Auntie Pamela, Tiger. What's the matter?"

"What's the matter?!" Pamela's voice went up an octave. "You ask me what the matter is when the chimney has fallen off my roof and a tree has fallen on Nick's barn and

77

the Hannibals' farmhouse is flooded and Railway Street looks like the Grand Canal in Venice and Smoky Bacon has fallen off the station wall…"

"Smoky has fallen off the station wall?" Tiger gasped theatrically, and would have clasped her hands to her heart except that she was holding the phone. "Is he…?"

"No, don't be silly, Lily. He's just a bit confused and he has a bump on his forehead."

"But what was he doing on the station wall?"

"Tiger, it's not really a good time to talk. It had something to do with a cat. Anyway, we're all moving up to the Old Jam Factory and, as if we haven't got enough on our plate, the Wolves are revolting."

In the background, Lily could hear Sweetness and Light singing in their high reedy voices.

We shall, we shall,
We shall not be moved,
Just like a tree that's standing
by the waterside,
We shall not be moved.

"Why are they revolting? What's the matter with them? Why are they singing?"

"They're, um, distressed."

"Like damsels in storybooks needing to be rescued by knights in shining armour?"

Pamela let out a long breath. "In a way."

79

"But, Auntie Pamela, we were just about to go to your house with our things. What'll we do now?"

"You'd better come to the Old Jam Factory with the rest of us. But first, tell your mum to go and get the Wolves."

Her voice became very crackly and the phone screen went black. And when Tiger tried to ring her back, there was no signal.

"Mum," Tiger shouted, "we have to go NOW. We have to go on a rescue mission."

"OK," Mum shouted from upstairs. "I'll just get my raincoat. Take the overnight bag and my door keys – they're on the table. And Rosie had better come, too. Put her on her lead."

Rosie pricked up her ears at the sound of the word "lead" and splashed off excitedly towards the front door. Tiger grabbed the overnight bag and splashed after her.

Chapter 7

Squalls of horizontal rain whipped their faces as Tiger, Mum and Rosie set off to rescue the Wolves. Raindrops trickled under their collars and down their necks. The flood water swirled around their toes, and then by gradual degrees, their ankles, calves and knees until with a chilly tickly gush, it poured into their wellies.

On the way, they passed embattled groups of neighbours, all of them bent double with heavy suitcases or bulging plastic bags like the one Tiger was carrying.

Spanners Murphy came trundling along at the back of the line looking like a refugee running away from a war with his belongings in a cart, except that it wasn't a cart he was pushing but a wheelbarrow – and Smoky Bacon was in it. Smoky looked dazed. He was very white, his peaked hat had fallen over one eye and his moustache was soaking wet and crestfallen.

"Whatever you do, don't let that new fellow eat the pigeon," he called out to Tiger.

"Nobody eats pigeon, Smoky."

"Maestro might. He's always hungry. Came on the train last week. First class carriage, if you don't mind."

Spanners shook his head sadly. "Smoky is talking real funny since he fell off the wall."

"He must be concussed," said Mum, straightening Smoky's hat. "Smoky, you're going to be all right. Don't worry…"

"That's another thing," said Spanners, lowering his voice. "How can we get an ambulance here with all the phones down. We're cut off, Vicky."

"Tiger, listen to me." Smoky caught Tiger's elbow and pressed his stationmaster's whistle into her hand. "Take this. Maestro always comes looking for his dinner when he hears me blowing the whistle when the train comes in." He sank back, exhausted.

Mum bit her lip. "Where's Pam?" she asked.

"She jumped ship and went to help Rita set things up at the Old Jam Factory. Piotr's waiting for you at the post office to rescue Sweetness and Light."

"Great!" said Mum. "Good old Pam! We'll see you as soon as we can. Keep trying your phone and don't let Smoky fall asleep. Keep talking to him."

"Will do," said Spanners.

Chapter 8

When Tiger and Mum finally sploshed around the corner of Railway Street, they discovered that Auntie Pamela had not exaggerated.

It *was* like Venice – there weren't any gondolas, but there was some very unusual water traffic sailing up and down.

Streaky Bacon Junior was furiously paddling up the street on a large rubber tyre, balancing a hutch on his lap.

Streaky Bacon Senior was following him in an inflatable black dinghy.

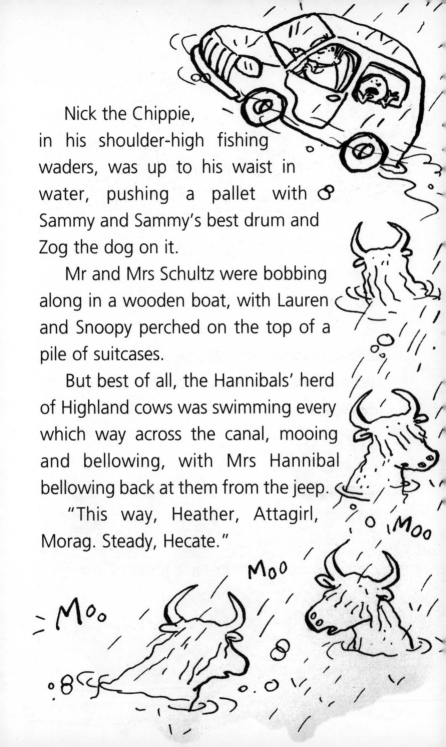

Nick the Chippie, in his shoulder-high fishing waders, was up to his waist in water, pushing a pallet with Sammy and Sammy's best drum and Zog the dog on it.

Mr and Mrs Schultz were bobbing along in a wooden boat, with Lauren and Snoopy perched on the top of a pile of suitcases.

But best of all, the Hannibals' herd of Highland cows was swimming every which way across the canal, mooing and bellowing, with Mrs Hannibal bellowing back at them from the jeep.

"This way, Heather, Attagirl, Morag. Steady, Hecate."

Moo

Moo

Moo

"Tiger. *Cześć!*" Piotr glided towards Tiger and Mum in a punt, expertly slaloming between the protesting cows. "Hop in, Vicky. Let's hope the Wolves listen to you. They won't budge for any of us."

"I don't believe this," Mum wailed, as she, Tiger and Rosie climbed aboard. "I can't swim and I hate boats! I've always hated boats!"

"Oh, come on, Mum, don't be such a landlubber! What does a sailor care for a rocky sea? Let's rescue the fair Damsels in Distress. Aaaar. Aaaar."

Tiger hadn't been messing about on a boat since she and Sammy had made the pallet-raft and gone down the river like Huckleberry Finn in search of adventure last summer.

"Ahoy there, Psammy!" she roared. "Love your pallet! Pretend we're pirates besieging Venice and I'm the leader of the flotilla. Come on, me hearties. All hands on deck. Cut the jib, Lauren! Splice the mainbrace, Streaky! Row, row, row, your boats, gently down the stream, merrily, merrily, merrily, merrily, life is but a dream, tra—"

"Lily," said Mum, pulling at her sleeve, "SIT DOWN. If you rock the boat once more, I will KILL you."

Tiger sat down.

The Damsels in Distress were leaning out of the upstairs window of the post office, looking down their sharp noses at all the hugger-mugger below. However, as soon as they realized that the pirates' flotilla of dinghy, rubber tyre, pallet, canoe and punt had come to rescue them, they immediately set up a tuneless dirge about "keeping the home fires burning."

Vicky, who was turning Kermit-green, had to shout loudly to be heard above the wolfish din. "Ladies, you really must come with us; it's not safe and you'll catch your death of cold…"

"You'll never take us from our home," Sweetness (or maybe it was Light) shouted back. "We didn't move out in the blitz and we're not moving out now. Never, never! Over our dead bodies!"

This unfortunately made Piotr and Mum and the Schultzes and Nick the Chippie wish they really were dead bodies, instead of just being two annoying Wolves who had to be saved whether they liked it or not.

"What a cranky, ungrateful…" Nick said.

"…stubborn…" said Piotr.

"…pair of old crones." Mr Schultz finished the sentence.

"Nevertheless," said Mum, looking greener, "we can't just leave them. Can one

of you please come up with an idea? I have to get back on dry land or I am going to be sick."

That was when Tiger Lily had another of her ingenious ideas.

She stood up (carefully balancing herself so as not to rock the boat).

"Listen up, Miss Wolf," she shouted at Sweetness (or possibly it was Light). She was very careful to address a point between the two sisters' cheesecutter noses. "I know it's a lot to ask, but since you're most probably an expert, what with being in the *blitz* and knowing about *evacuees*," she stumbled on, clutching blindly at the strange words she had read in *Carrie's War*, "and sugar *rations* and *blackouts* and *sirens* and *wardens*, that's it, wardens. We'd like you and your sister to be our wardens and set up your headquarters in the Old Jam Factory."

"Wardens?" The twins pursed their thin lips. "You want us to take charge of the evacuation?"

Tiger and Mum and Piotr nodded.

"It would be our job to call out the rescue services?"

Tiger and Mum and Piotr nodded again.

"And we'd sound the All Clear?"

"Yes, yes," said Mum and Piotr.

"So," said Tiger, rummaging in her pocket for Smoky's whistle, "you'll need this. We'll get you the helmets with a W on them as soon as we can."

Sweetness and Light exchanged a look. They dipped their chins. "You can count on us to do our duty," they said.

93

A great cheer went up the length of the Grand Canal.

"Tiger, you're ingenious!" said Mum, and Piotr, quick as a Venetian gondolier, splashed off into the post office before the Wolves could change their minds.

He was on his way down the stairs with the second twin over his shoulder when all of a sudden Sweetness (or was it Light?) let out a wail of despair.

"The cats!" she yelled. "We can't abandon the cats."

So it took another ten minutes to scoop up all the post office cats (including one with a scar on its face that Tiger found curled up asleep in the laundry basket). Tiger Lily and Mum counted them into cardboard boxes and Sammy and Nick ferried them over to

Mr Hannibal, who had very conveniently come back from dropping off the cows at the Old Playground and promised to put them somewhere secure. Which, given his track record of losing wild boar, not to mention his roaming peacocks and walkabout goats, wasn't very reassuring. The Hannibals were always losing their animals.

Then things took a turn for the worse.

Tiger and Mum were standing up, helping settle the twins aboard when Mr Hannibal revved his engine and sent a tidal wave rolling down the canal.

"Waaaah!" Tiger shouted as the wash hit the side of the punt.

As she teetered backwards, she reached out and grabbed Mum's shoulder. The boat rocked violently from side to side.

Mum lost her balance.

"Lily!" she screamed, as she did a backward flip and fell into Streaky's tyre.

"Ow! Get off!" screamed Streaky, as his tyre upended and he and Mum fell into the chilly waters of the Venetian lagoon.

One of the twins blew a loud piercing blast on Smoky's whistle.

"SOS!" shouted the other one. "Civilians overboard. Call out the emergency services."

As Nick the Chippie and Piotr answered their call, Tiger remembered Mum's last words.

If you rock the boat once more, Tiger, I will KILL you.

Chapter 9

Meanwhile, Miss Monica Caramelo was sitting alone in the dark in the Bay Tree Café, feeling rather sorry for herself.

Granny Rita had popped out earlier to take some candles to the Old Jam Factory.

"I'll be back in a jiffy," she had said, as she was leaving. "I don't expect you'll want to go out in this weather, but if you do, use the back door. The key for the front one jams when there's a power cut. Make yourself at home. Help yourself to anything you fancy."

That had been hours ago. Since then the

storm had got worse and worse. The wind shrieked. The rain lashed against the café window. Bolts of thunder rumbled and crashed over the village. It grew darker and darker. Nobody came to ask how she was.

Miss Caramelo sighed, remembering the blue skies and the sunny orange groves she had left behind. "The Middle of Nowhere in November! What was I thinking of?"

She cleared a small peephole in the condensation on the window and peered out.

"Hello!" she exclaimed. "What's this?"

A strange procession was making its way past the café. There were two men carrying what looked like a dead body on a plank of wood and behind them, a cortège of wet, bedraggled women and children. Trailing along at the very back was a limping dog and

99

– Monica put her face a little closer to her peephole – yes, it was the book girl, Tiger Lily, carrying a large black sack.

They trudged past, solemnly climbed the steps of the Old Jam Factory and disappeared through the Stage Door.

"Gracious to goodness, it's like something from one of those tragic Irish plays my grandpoppa was so fond of. Imagine putting on a show to entertain the poor folks who have been flooded out of their homes. Isn't that just so noble of

them?" Miss Caramelo clapped her hands. "I shall simply have to go and see it."

Miss Caramelo applied some lipstick, collected her coat and her poppy hat and checked that she had everything she needed in her carpet bag. Then she banged the café door shut and, despite the hammering rain, walked in a lady-like fashion across the square. As she had told Granny Rita earlier, Caramelos are always cool, calm and collected and they never run.

At the entrance to the theatre, she stopped to shake the raindrops off her umbrella and gasped.

"Oh my!"

Pathways of glimmering tea-lights radiated in all directions. They snaked around the Old Jam Factory's higgledy-piggledy collection of rickety patio seats, mismatched dining-chairs, kitchen stools and swivelling desk-chairs. Some of the evacuees were setting up makeshift camps wherever they could find a space, pumping up inflatable beds and unrolling sleeping bags. The candlelight

threw their shadows on the walls, making them look like grizzly bears padding around their caves in bulky overcoats.

"I can see that this is a most uncommon theatre," Miss Caramelo said to herself. "If I were asked to describe it, I would say it glows. It's magic. I must find the acting troupe at once and find out when the performance begins."

She set off towards the stage, wending her way through the chattering crowds, but as she passed an old cracked leather sofa, she heard a sniff and a sob followed by another sniff. And another sob.

The noises were coming from Tiger Lily.

She was curled up, face hidden in the cushions of the sofa. Rosie was sitting beside her, her long face resting on Tiger's feet.

"Is that you, Miss Tiger Lily? What are you doing?"

Tiger Lily didn't move. "I'm hiding."

"Hiding? Who are you hiding from?"

"Everyone. But especially Mum. If she finds me, she is going to KILL me."

"You'd better start at the beginning," said Miss Caramelo.

So Tiger did.

Chapter 10

The Tale of the Wrong Bag

As told to Miss Monica Caramelo by Tiger Lily on the Eve of her Execution

…Tiger Lily drew a breath. "When the Warden Wolves were getting on board, I rocked the boat again and made Mum and Streaky Junior and his rabbit fall into the Grand Canal. Piotr managed to pull Mum out with his punting pole and Sammy grabbed Streaky's hutch – but Streaky Junior had disappeared!

"Nick the Chippie had to hold his nose and dive under the pallet to look for him. Everyone held their breath to help until Nick reappeared with Streaky in his arms. Streaky was choking and choking and his arm was COVERED IN BLOOD and it was BROKEN.

"Mr Schultz and Piotr and Mr Hannibal all tried to call an ambulance, but their mobile phones were still not working so the ambulance cannot come and if Streaky dies, it will be my fault. And Smoky most probably will die, too.

"But then things got a million times worse.

107

Nick laid Streaky on the pallet and pushed it to the water's edge and then he and Piotr carried it, like it was a stretcher, all the way here to the Old Jam Factory."

"Oh my," said Miss Caramelo, clutching her heart. "And to think I saw you all passing the café and thought you were putting on a play."

"Did you really?" Tiger Lily perked up for a minute. "I wish I was on the stage like you. I have always wanted to be a heroine." She clutched her heart.

"You were going to tell me why things got a million times worse…" prompted Miss Caramelo.

"Well, Mum was dripping and fuming and shivering and looking murderous and the Warden Wolves linked arms with her, one on each side, and

marched her off behind the pallet and everybody else walked behind them in a procession, and I tried not to think of:

(1) Streaky dying and me being sent to prison

(2) Mum dying and me being an orphan

(3) Mum not dying but killing me.

109

"Whichever way it turned out, it was not good."

Tiger sniffed.

"Then the Next Very Bad Thing happened."

"The Next Very Bad Thing?"

"When we got here, Mum said, 'At least I have a dry set of clothes to change into.'" Tiger Lily's eyes slid to the plastic bag at the end of the sofa. She sniffed again.

"Go on," said Miss Monica.

"But when I opened the stupid bag to get her clothes, it was THE WRONG BAG. It was the bag of Mum's junk, all the clothes she was going to give away.

"And when Mum saw what I had done, she shouted, 'Lily, how could you be so SILLY? I could KILL you.' So I rushed off home for the

RIGHT BAG, but I couldn't get in because I had forgotten to take the keys when Mum told me to…"

Tears rolled down Tiger's face and she could hardly speak for sobbing.

"My life is not worth living. My mum is going to kill me. Say goodbye to all my friends." She put her hand to her forehead the way tragic heroines do. "Please take care of my dog."

"Oh honey, what a fine mess you have gotten yourself into!" Miss Monica nodded at the bag at Tiger's feet. "Is that the Wrong Bag?"

Tiger Lily nodded back.

Miss Caramelo took a peek inside. "Miss Tiger, I don't think this is the Wrong Bag at all. I think this bag is just perfect. Where is your mum?"

"Backstage," Tiger Lily sniffed.

Miss Caramelo undid the catch of her carpet bag and took out a handkerchief.

"Miss Tiger," she said, "sniffing is not ladylike. Give your nose a good blow and follow me! We have a show to put on."

Chapter 11

Backstage, the evacuees were huddled in a circle around a gas heater. Zog and Snoopy were fast asleep. Streaky Bacon was wrapped up in a blanket, dozing in his father's arms and looking as white as a Halloween ghost.

Lauren was helping Sammy to dry his best drum.

"Sammy," she asked, "where is Tiger? Why is she taking so long to come back with her mum's dry clothes? Can you hear a fluttery noise?"

The Warden Wolves, Granny, Piotr, Spanners and Nick were milling around Smoky Bacon, who seemed to have taken a turn for the worse, muttering nonsense about sending home the bacon.

Mum was sitting on a bench, wrapped up in the stage curtain and still looking murderous, even though Auntie Pamela was towelling her hair dry and singing to keep her spirits up.

The minute that Tiger and Rosie appeared, she jumped to her feet. "At last, Lily! Have you got the Right Bag?"

"No," said Tiger, in a very small voice. "I've locked us out..."

Before Mum could fly off the handle, Monica Caramelo stepped out of the wings.

"Miss Monica!" Granny exclaimed, "I'd forgotten all about you! As you can see, things got out of hand... Oh!" She clapped her hands to her face. "You didn't..."

"Didn't what, Miss Rita?"

"Didn't leave through the café door?"

Granny's face fell as Miss Monica turned a little red.

"But, Miss Monica, that means until the electricity comes back on we're locked out too..."

Miss Caramelo drew herself up to her formidable height.

"My dear Miss Rita, children, ladies and gentlemen," she declared. "My grandpoppa, a man who was proud to say that he came from The Middle of Nowhere, well, he had an expression when any kind of disaster

116

struck. When the airline lost our props or the scenery fell over or when his toast fell on the buttered side, he used to say, 'The only thing a person can do is RISE ABOVE IT!' So that is what I suggest we all do. We will rise above the misfortunes of the locked doors and the mixed-up bags. Tiger, will you be a darling and pass these around…"

Miss Monica started pulling things out of the Wrong Bag – the ski suit, the saris, the jellaba, the fez, the Japanese flag, the pantomime cat costume and the fake fur coat.

"Vicky, this ski suit looks so cosy... Mr Bacon Senior, this will make the most perfect turban for your sore head..." She took a length of silk sari and with a few deft magic twists turned it into an elaborate headdress, which Tiger popped on Smoky's head. "And until we can get that arm of yours in plaster, this will make an excellent sling." She gently wrapped the Japanese flag around Streaky's broken arm.

"Lauren, I do believe you will look the cat's pyjamas in this. Nick the Chippie, this jellaba has your name written all over it. Sammy, I always think a musician looks good in a fez.

118

Miss Rita, you have had a very trying day today, but tonight you are the belle of the ball. You will look the bees' knees in this fur."

Tiger Lily raced around the evacuees, handing out their new clothes. Mesmerized by Miss Monica, they put them on without a single protest. Even Sammy liked his fez.

Only the Warden Wolves seemed a bit miffed, until Tiger Lily fished out the two safari hats from the bottom of the bag.

"Perfect," she announced. "Just like wardens' hats but nicer."

"Now, if we are all set…" Miss Caramelo opened her carpet bag and drew out a small kettle, a mini gas cooker, a tea caddy, a small tin of sugar and a box of sugared almonds. "…I am sure we could all appreciate a good old-fashioned cup of tea."

"What is that noise?" Lauren interrupted. "Is that Streaky's rabbit? Do rabbits make that sort of fluttery noise?"

"What noise?"

"That noise."

For only the second time in her life, Lauren said something that wasn't a question.

Everyone listened.

"That's Homie," said Streaky Junior,

120

opening his eyes. "He came
on the train at
lunchtime
and now he
wants to
go home."

"Who's
Homie?"

Streaky's
dad opened
the door of
the rabbit
hutch that
wasn't a rabbit
hutch at all and
took out...

"A pigeon?!" chorused everyone.

"It's not just any pigeon," said Streaky
Junior. "That's my uncle's best racing pigeon.
He brings him up on the train and then we
release him and he flies home. He's brilliant."

121

Homie the pigeon hopped on to Streaky's finger and cocked an eye.

"A racing pigeon!" Tiger Lily's eyes glowed. "I have an idea! Can pigeons fly in the dark?"

"Of course!" said Streaky. "Everyone knows that."

"Quick," said Tiger, "I need a piece of paper and a pen and an elastic band. What is your uncle's name?"

"Sidney, but everyone calls him Rashers."

Miss Monica forgot that Caramelos are always cool, calm and collected and ran to open her carpet bag.

"Miss Tiger, I have a notebook and pen," she said, holding them up with a flourish.

"Here," said Sammy, "lean on my drum."

Tiger Lily tore out a page and wrote:

122

Dear Mr Rashers Bacon,

This is an SOS. The Middle of Nowhere is flooded. Please send an ambulance at once to the Old Jam Factory to save the Bacons.

Thank you to you and Homie.

Tiger Lily x

When she had finished, Streaky Senior tied the note to Homie's leg with an elastic band that Auntie Pamela had found in her pocket, and then the Warden Wolves blew their whistle.

"Follow us," they said. "No running. No shouting. Form an orderly line. Mind the candles."

Streaky, with Homie perched on his good arm, and Tiger and all the other evacuees fell into line behind the Wolves and they walked

through the pathway of tea-lights to the
EMERGENCY EXIT.

Streaky patted the feathers of Homie's
neck and said in Pigeon, "Fly away, Homie,"
which sounded a bit like "Hooh-hrooo,
Homie, drruoo-uu."

A loud cheer went up as Homie took off.
He flew out into the storm and soared high
up into the sky until he was nothing more
than a tiny black speck.

"How long will he be?" asked Lauren. "What will we do while we're waiting for the ambulance? Can anyone hear a cat miaowing?"

Mum looked at Tiger.

"Lily, do you remember Scheherazade?"

Tiger nodded.

"And do you still have the veil I gave you?"

Tiger pulled it out of her pocket.

"Then why don't you tell us all a story? It's a perfect night for telling stories."

"In that case," said Miss Monica, having the last word, "I would be most obliged if you gentlemen could fetch the old *chaise longue* for Mr Smoky to lie down on. I do believe there is an Arabian king in this story." She clapped her hands together. "On stage, everybody."

FINAL CALL

Chapter 12

When everyone had found somewhere to sit, Tiger Lily began.

"On the night of the Great Wind, the Persian King Smoky Bacon was comfortably resting on his *chaise longue*, wearing a new silk turban. Please remember, Smoky was not the cruel king who killed wives, but the most beloved king the land had ever known. Lauren, the king's favourite cat, was curled up at his feet and Rosie, his champion greyhound, lay on the floor beside him, keeping him safe from all harm.

"The court musician, Sami Bin Nikacheepee, also known as Psammy, squatted on the floor with his best drum, waiting for His Majesty's summons to play.

"On either side of the couch, the viziers – they were the king's most important advisers – Nickacheepee and Spanners Mur-fee, sat in attendance, watching over the king, who had not been well that day. Fortunately, the Royal Physician was on his way in a magic flying machine.

"There were also visitors in court that night, taking refuge from the storm. Piotr, the Pied Piper from Poland, was there and so was Streaky, the Artist from the Land of the Rising Sun, who lay eating perfumed sugar almonds, with his broken arm wrapped in a Japanese sling.

Last but not least, Miss Monica Caramelo, the Strolling Player from the New World, sat on a bench with the three Wise Women – the Cook and her two daughters, the Travelling Book Woman and the Singing Hairdresser.

"When they fell silent, Scheherazade began her first story, 'The Tale of the Very Foolish Daughter'."

Once upon a time there was a Travelling Book Woman who was as beautiful as the day and she was beloved in all the many lands that she had ever visited, from whence she brought many exotic raiments—

"Can't you talk properly?" interrupted Sammy. "I can't understand a word you're saying."

Tiger Lily sighed. "She had a lovely face and she had been all over the world and she never saw a scratchy jellaba or a silly hat or a hideous raincoat that she couldn't do without. OK?"

"Why didn't you say that in the first place?" said Sammy.

"I have to talk this way. I'm not me talking. I'm Scheherazade, for goodness' sake." Tiger straightened her veil and started again.

The Travelling Book Woman lived in a cottage in One-End Street with her Foolish Daughter, Silly Lily.

Silly Lily was called Lily because she was as long and thin as the letters L and I, but the musician Sami bin Nikacheepee also called her Tiger because her hair was as red as the stripes of the tigers that roamed in the royal menagerie. So it came to pass that everyone called her Tiger Lily, except the Travelling Book Woman with the lovely face who just called her Lily or, more usually, Silly.

One day the Very Foolish Daughter was running under the railway bridge, holding her nose because of the pooey smell of goat droppings left there by the roaming goats from Hannibals' farm, when she heard a small voice say:

"Alas! Alack the day I wanted to be famous!"

And when Silly Lily gazed in the dark cobwebby place where the voice was coming from, what did she see but a creature so thin that, verily, its ribs were sticking through its skin. When the Very Foolish Daughter's eyes had got used to the gloom, she saw that the creature was a dog, but the poor thing had nothing but a stump where her fourth leg should have been.

"What is your name?" quoth Silly Lily. "What has brought you to this stinky place?" and the dog blinked her long eyelashes and laid her long face on the Very Foolish Daughter's hand and she began to speak.

And here followeth The Tale of the Greyhound, in her own words.

Tiger paused to take a cup of tea and a biscuit from Warden Sweetness (or perhaps it was Warden Light).

"How am I doing, Sami Bin Nickacheepee?"

"OK," said her court musician, a bit doubtfully, "better – but there are still too many quoths and followeths – and when do I get to play my drum?"

"I'll tell you what," Tiger said. "Why don't you start each story with a drum roll and come in every time I say, 'Music please, Maestro'?"

At the word "Maestro", there was a loud *miaow miaow* and a cat appeared from out of the shadows. It was a black and white cat, with a z-shaped scar on its cheek.

"Maestro!" exclaimed Smoky, raising himself on his elbow. "You're safe."

"No, Smoky, that's our cat, Zorro," said Piotr. "He's very fond of beetroot, believe it or not."

"No," said Lauren, "isn't that my new cat, Harry?"

"Don't be ridiculous!" said the Warden Wolves together. "It's our new cat, Fifi."

"Fifi?" everyone chorused. "That's ridiculous! It's a TOM CAT!"

The cat boldly gazed at the circle of evacuees for a long minute.

"It's definitely Maestro," said Smoky, "I told you – he arrived in The Middle of Nowhere one day last week. Travelled first class, if you don't mind. He comes looking for food when I blow my whistle."

"Nonsense! That's Zorro!" insisted Piotr. "Look at the z-shaped scar on his cheek."

"It's Fifi! We'd know her anywhere," said the Warden Wolves.

"Harry!" said Lauren.

Tiger Lily put down her teacup and adjusted her veil.

"*Viziers, arrest that cat at once,*" she called out as if she was Scheherazade again, "*and bring it before the Bench.*"

"But Tiger, weren't you going to tell us the story of the greyhound?" asked Lauren.

"This is the way Scheherazade tells stories," Tiger said. "She puts stories inside other stories. I'll come back to Rosie later."

"Gracious to goodness," exclaimed Miss Monica, reaching for her carpet bag. "I'd better get out my knitting. I can see this could be a long night."

Chapter 13

The First Tale of the Cat

Nickacheepee and Spanners Mur-fee set the cat before the Wise Women on the Bench, where it insolently began to wash behind its ears.

Scheherazade held the lapels of her coat and bowed to the Bench.

"You see here before you," she began, striding up and down before the Court, "a Master of Disguise, a Cat of Many Parts. Some of you may have seen this cat already today, sheltering in the bay tree, behaving suspiciously in the café and hiding in a laundry basket. Now it has strolled in here, cool as a cucumber, miaowing for its dinner." She stopped in front of the cat and gave it a hard stare.

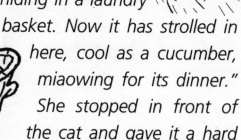

"Why do I know it has come looking for its dinner? Because, ladies and gentlemen, it heard the Wardens blow the Stationmaster's whistle when Homie was leaving and, right on cue, it arrived here. Don't you remember Lauren heard miaowing!"

The court gasped. The cat turned pale.

"Yes!" said Scheherazade, "I accuse this cat of being Maestro, the cat that caused the king to fall off his wall."

"I never did, Your Honour," the cat stammered. "I wasn't there. You're mixing me up with some other cat."

"Pray then, tell us your name, Cat."

The cat coughed. "Sorry," it croaked. "I have a fishbone stuck in my throat. I cannot speak."

"Cat," said Scheherazade, "I further accuse you of the use of pseudonyms. That's sood-nim, with a silent p. Do you know what a pseudonym is?"

The cat looked blank.

"A pseudonym is a false name! An adopted name! I put it to you, Cat, that you are an impostor!"

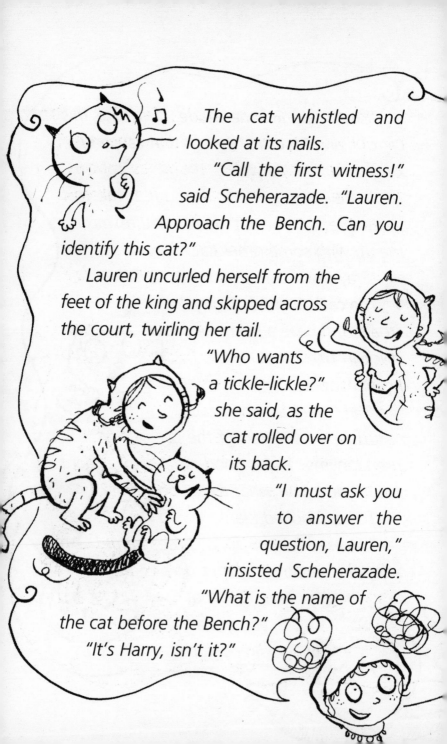

The cat whistled and looked at its nails.

"Call the first witness!" said Scheherazade. "Lauren. Approach the Bench. Can you identify this cat?"

Lauren uncurled herself from the feet of the king and skipped across the court, twirling her tail.

"Who wants a tickle-lickle?" she said, as the cat rolled over on its back.

"I must ask you to answer the question, Lauren," insisted Scheherazade.

"What is the name of the cat before the Bench?"

"It's Harry, isn't it?"

"Harry? Is that your name, Cat? Tell us now or we will throw you out into the rain."

The cat's eyes grew round as saucers. "Not the rain," it croaked, "I'm allergic to rain."

The Wolves cleared their throats. "If we could have a word, Your Honour," they said together. "We know this cat."

At this, the shameless cat bounced towards the twins and rubbed its head against their outstretched hands.

"This cat is not Harry," said the first Wolf, who might have been Sweetness.

"Nor is it Maestro," said the second Wolf, who might have been Light.

"It's our cat, Fifi."

"Nonsense!" said the Pied Piper. From beneath his coat of many colours, he drew forth a jar and pulled out a crinkled round of pickled beetroot.

At the sight of this, the cat walked, no it raced towards the Pied Piper and did a figure of eight around his legs. Its purr almost drowned out the noise of the wind outside.

"I rest my case," said the Pied Piper. "This is Zorro, the beetroot-eating cat."

At once, all the owners of the cat began to shout at one another. The cat hissed. The dogs barked.

"It's Fifi."

"It's Zorro."

"It's Harry."

"It's Maestro."

The king groaned.

"Silence in court," shouted Scheherazade. "You are giving the king a headache. Prithee, what is the judgement of the Bench?"

"Guilty as charged!" said the Travelling Book Woman. "The cat is an impostor."

"Out into the rain with it at once," said the Singing Hairdresser.

"Off with its head, I say," cried Miss Monica, without looking up from her knitting.

The cat held up its paws. "OK, OK," he purred. "Keep your hair on. I'll tell you who I am."

Chapter 14

The Second Tale of the Cat

"My name's Hernando. I grew up on the docks in a dark secluded spot called Hernando's Hideaway."

"Hernando's Hideaway, A-way," sang Sami Bin Nikacheepee, banging his drum.

"I wasn't a bad cat – I just got in with a bad crowd. Every time a fish went missing or a bin was overturned the neighbours said:

'Where's Hernando?' I took the blame for everything. I was the fall guy.

"Then my luck changed. One day, I was running across a hot tin roof when a sailor called up to me. 'Hey, Cat, do you want a job?'

"Whaddya know – he wanted me to be the Company Cat. The Company Cat! On a whaling boat out of Valparaiso – that's in Chile! It was a dream come true! *Otro Mundo Es Posible. Another world is possible.*

"Ladies of the Bench, I took to the sailing life like a kitten to cream – even though some of the sailors I met were as likely to kick me off their bunk as throw me a fish-head. But I saw the world – and you know how much fun that is!"

The cat winked at the Travelling Book Woman. "I worked on Norwegian trawlers, Basque fishing-boats, Saudi tankers, I got all the flags."

"Why then did you stop travelling?" asked the Travelling Book Woman.

The cat sighed. "It was a dame. I was distracted by the flashing green eyes of a Spanish lady cat, washing her feet by candlelight and fell head over heels in love. I decided to settle down, think about having kittens, but I had hardly hung up my souwester when the señorita tells me that visitors, like fish, shouldn't hang around for more than three days. 'Here's your hat,' she says, and shows me the door. It looked like my luck had finally run out. I was running short of lives.

"Early the next morning, I woke up in the railway station. A train was standing on the platform. The First Class carriage door was open. I did not hesitate. I boarded the train for The Middle of Nowhere."

The cat stopped and looked at the circle of listening faces.

"And I have to say, hand on my heart, I feel soooo at home here."

"In whose home?" Scheherazade said sternly. "Answer the question."

The cat drew out a medallion on a chain from under its tangled chest fur and held it up for the Court to read.

Maestro,
The Railway Station,
Tel: MON 44

"So you admit you are Maestro, the cat that nearly killed the Old King?" Scheherazade gave the cat a hard stare.

The cat gave her a look back.

"I admit nothing. I have never been Zorro, Fifi, Harry or Maestro or any of those other pseudonyms with a silent p. I do not adopt names – people give them to me. Yes," it stuck out its chest, "I am a cat – I empty litter bins, I sing at night. I allow the Girl Who Asks The Questions to tickle my tummy. I eat the beetroot only because the Singing Hairdresser buys it and the Pied Piper can't stand it. But," the cat clasped his paws to his heart, "if you don't believe me, throw me out into the storm…"

The wind moaned in the tall chimney of the Old Jam Factory. The rain drummed on the rooftops.

The lightning flashed.

The three Wise Women of the Bench and Miss Monica went into a huddle.

Everyone held their breath until Granny Rita's head bobbed up and she declared, "In the opinion of the Bench, the cat is free to go wherever he wants."

And with that, the cat walked off into the wings, waving goodbye with its tail.

"And that is the end of The Tale of the Cat," said Scheherazade.

"So now are you going to finish 'The Tale of the Greyhound', are you, are you?" Lauren asked. "What happened after Silly Lily found the greyhound under the bridge?"

"If it pleases the Court," said Scheherazade, "here followeth The Tale of the Greyhound, in her own words."

Chapter 15

The Tale of the Greyhound

Rosie the greyhound kowtowed before the king.

"When I were a young lass," she told the Court, "my greatest wish was to be a Celebrity... My name then was Brittany Chevron and I lived for the roar of the crowd. It was music to my ears as I strained at the slips, waiting for the starter's gun..."

Bang! went Sami Bin Nikacheepee.

"...and I was off, the blood pounding in my ears, my heart thumping, and a noise like drumming echoing around the ground as I hurtled past the finish line, all legs.

"I spent five years running after hares – the best years of my life.

"My trainer, Guvnor, took me hill-walking every day, and swimming on Friday nights to build up my shoulders. I had my own jacuzzi to soak in after the races. My picture was always in the newspapers. I had a glass cabinet full of gold cups. I was a star! I had it all!

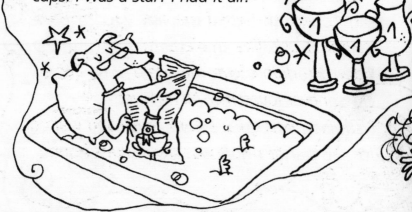

"Alas, I thought Guvnor loved me, but I was more hare-brained than the mechanical hares that I ran after."

Rosie, alias Brittany, paused to lick her missing limb, lost in her own thoughts.

"Brittany Chevron!" exclaimed Vizier Mur-fee. "I remember you. What a dog you were! What on earth happened?"

Rosie, alias Brittany, sighed. "It was the Spring Bank Holiday. Gold Cup Night at the Toffington Races. That's where it all went wrong. All it took was one bad corner, and my racing life was over. I was injured, no good to anyone. Redundant. That very same night, Guvnor tossed me out of the truck like a piece of litter. He didn't love me. He'd never loved me. All he loved was gold. I slunk away and waited to die. It was my darkest hour."

"I know what you mean," said Streaky. "Look at my arm. I may never be able to draw again."

"Don't be silly," said the Travelling Book Woman. "Every cloud has a silver lining, Streaky. You just can't see it yet."

"Princess's mum is right," said Rosie, also known as Brittany. "My accident was the best thing that ever could have happened to me, for Silly Lily, the Very Foolish Daughter, found me hiding in the stinky tunnel and took me back to the cluttered home in One-End Street where I live happily ever after. I have my own couch. What more could you ask for?"

She kowtowed to the Court and to the king. "If you please, Your Majesty, that is the end of my tale."

"Wonderful!" said the king.

"But it is not more wonderful than the tale of the artist Streaky from the Land of the Rising Sun," said Scheherazade.

Chapter 16

The Story of How Streaky
Learned Bird

One fine morning, the artist Streaky was strolling through the Zoological Gardens of a distant city when he came upon a large glass house. It was filled with palms and coconuts and giant banana trees. Birds with coats of many colours flitted among the branches.

The first thing that Streaky saw on entering was a beautiful parrot.

Its upper cheeks were yellow and the top of its head was lilac-blue. Its beak was grey and its eyes were golden, and when it took flight and spread its wings, it had deep blue wing tips. It was spectacular.

"Upon my word," quoth Streaky, "this is a member of the family Psittacidae *that I have never seen before." He immediately took out paints and paper and colouring pens and inks and set about drawing the exotic bird.*

While he drew, the parrot watched him and while it watched him, it sang:

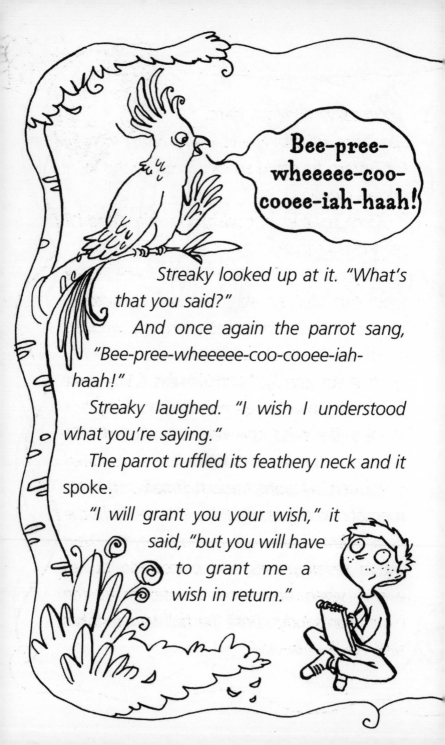

Bee-pree-wheeeee-coo-cooee-iah-haah!

Streaky looked up at it. "What's that you said?"

And once again the parrot sang, "Bee-pree-wheeeee-coo-cooee-iah-haah!"

Streaky laughed. "I wish I understood what you're saying."

The parrot ruffled its feathery neck and it spoke.

"I will grant you your wish," it said, "but you will have to grant me a wish in return."

Streaky blinked hard.
Speaking Bird could be very useful.
For a start, he could speak to Homie, his uncle's pigeon.

"First tell me your wish," he said, "and I'll see what I can do."

"My wish is to fly to Mexico where I once lived, but alas, all we lories and cockatoos, macaws and lovebirds and parrots have been imprisoned in this glasshouse."

"But you can fly," said Streaky. "Why can't you just fly away when nobody is looking?"

"It's like this," the parrot explained. "By day, we are under constant watch, surrounded by keepers. At night, the watchman comes. He has lost so many animals that now he locks the door with seven keys and places the keys within seven purses and places the purses within seven bags and sits sentry at the watchman's lodge until the bell tower strikes seven bells at dawn."

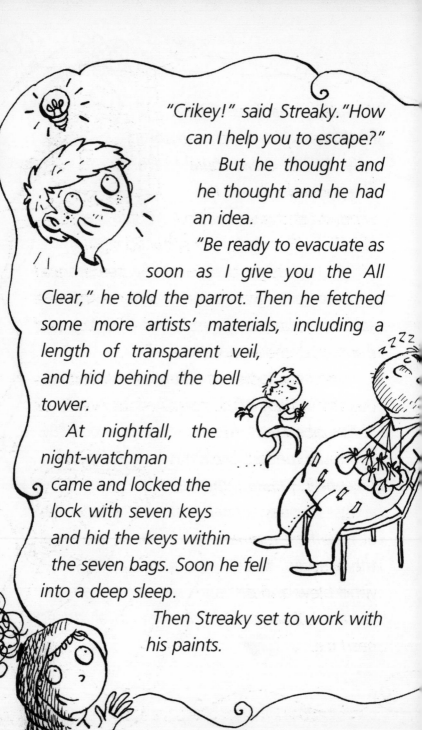

"Crikey!" said Streaky. "How can I help you to escape?"

But he thought and he thought and he had an idea.

"Be ready to evacuate as soon as I give you the All Clear," he told the parrot. Then he fetched some more artists' materials, including a length of transparent veil, and hid behind the bell tower.

At nightfall, the night-watchman came and locked the lock with seven keys and hid the keys within the seven bags. Soon he fell into a deep sleep.

Then Streaky set to work with his paints.

When the seven bells rang, the night-watchman's wife came downstairs. She looked out of the window and saw that all was fine. There was the splendid sight of the glasshouse, with its palms and coconuts and giant banana trees and, here and there, the turquoise wing of a lory and the scarlet cheek of a lovebird.

Then she looked a little closer. What was the tiny writing in the corner of the window? She rubbed at the windowpane but the tiny writing did not go away – it was outside. She opened the window. The wind blew and a curtain billowed into her face.

There was a veil hanging in front of the watchman's lodge, painted with a perfect copy of the birdhouse with the palms and the coconuts and the bananas and the lories and the cockatoos and the parrots roosting in the branches. And in one corner, in tiny writing, the signature of the artist. Streaky.

Streaky

The night-watchman's wife pushed aside the painted veil. There was the real birdhouse and, oh my, a window was broken and all the Psittacidae were gone.

"Oi, Hannibal," bellowed the night-watchman's wife – for Hannibal was the night-watchman's name – "you featherhead! You've gone and let all the birds escape!"

"And that," said Scheherazade, when the laughter stopped, "is The Story of How Streaky Learned Bird."

"Shhh," said Lauren. "What's that noise?"

Everybody hushed. It was a humming noise that got louder and louder and a whirring that got closer and closer.

"It's a HELICOPTER!" shouted Sammy. "A helicopter ambulance! Homie made it! Hurray for Homie! Everything is going to be all right!"

The entire Court rose to their feet like a flock of exotic brightly-coloured *Psittacidae*. They were hopping and dancing and whooping and giving high fives.

"I'm going to fly," Streaky yelled. "My wish has come true, Tiger! I'm really going to fly."

The Warden Wolves blew their whistle.

"This way, please. Follow us. Form an orderly line. No running. Viziers, open the Emergency Door."

Lauren and Tiger Lily helped the Persian King to his feet and took him by the hand; Streaky and his dad and Sammy and his dad fell in behind and the Cook and her two daughters, the Travelling Book Woman and the Singing Hairdresser, the Pied Piper, Miss Monica and everybody else followed them.

They emerged, blinking like moles, into the morning light.

Sometime during the night, while Tiger was telling her stories, the storm had blown away. The rain had stopped, the sky was streaked with pink and an air ambulance was hovering above the square.

As soon as it touched the ground, the door opened and a pair of ambulance men jumped out, carrying a stretcher.

"Yee-Hi, Tiger!" shouted Spanners, doing the Cajun Walk. "You have saved the Bacons. What a girl!"

Tiger turned to her mum. "Does that mean you're not going to kill me?"

"Kill you? Why would I kill you?" Mum said, all memory of boat rocking and Wrong Bags forgotten. "You are the most ingenious daughter in the world!"

"Yes," said Miss Monica, having the last word, "I do believe that Miss Tiger Lily, with her acting and her storytelling talents, is most probably related to the Caramelo clan. She is certainly a Heroine for All Seasons."

But that is not quite the end of the story.

Chapter 17

Two weeks later, Tiger was lying on her bed writing a story in her notebook.

"Listen to this, Mum," she called down to her mum, who was painting the kitchen.

"It's Scheherazade's last tale from the Book of the Very Foolish Daughter, Silly Lily. It's called 'The Tale of the Letter'."

"Go for it, Tiger," said Mum, taking a rest on the top of the stepladder.

"Miss Monica left The Middle of Nowhere on the helicopter with Smoky and Streaky.

Two days later, Streaky 'the Birdman' Bacon came home with a fully-illustrated arm, all painted with blue-faced lories and lovebirds and parrots and macaws.

A week later, Smoky Bacon came home, too.

There wasn't a peep out of Miss Monica about researching the Caramelo family tree, and the Travelling Book Woman said she always knew that Miss Monica was just an old show-off.

Then one day, when the Cook was holding a little party to welcome back the Bacons, a messenger in royal livery arrived at the café bearing a letter for His Excellency of the High Visibility Jacket, Streaky Bacon Senior.

His Excellency read the letter aloud and this is what it said:

170

Dear Mr Bacon,

The American actress and director Monica Caramelo has drawn our attention to your delightful theatre, the Old Jam Factory, where she spent a magical time during the Night of the Great Wind.

Our film company, the award-winning All Seasons Productions, will be filming in your area in the spring. We would love to hire the Old Jam Factory for some indoor shoots. This is an exciting project with an international cast and an Oscar-winning director, which I am sure will be of great benefit to your community.

Our client can also offer some work for extras at the usual rates. We are particularly interested in meeting the girl who told the stories, the drummer, the birdman and the cat...

"You're joking, Lily, aren't you?" Mum interrupted.

"That never happened. It's a wind-up, isn't it? All Seasons Productions?"

Tiger Lily leaned over the stairs and grinned down at her.

"What do you think? Miss Monica said that I was a Heroine for All Seasons, remember? And she always has the last word."